To Babsy and Etta, I hope you find the magic in your life too!

Phyllis Borden

To:

My grandchildren, who inspire me:

Joey, Ethan, Ryan, Dylan, Max, and Sammy.

My children who have listened to my stories
and ideas endlessly.

My husband Paul, who has been my constant
support every step of the way.

MASCOT KIDS!®

www.amplifypublishinggroup.com

Lilly Esther, Queen of Magic

Second printing. This Mascot Kids edition printed in 2024.

For more information, please contact:
Mascot Kids, an imprint of Amplify Publishing Group
620 Herndon Parkway, Suite 220
Herndon, VA 20170
info@mascotbooks.com

Library of Congress Control Number: 2021923889

ISBN-13: 978-1-64543-833-5

Printed in Canada

Lilly Esther, Queen of Magic

Written by

Phyllis Bordo

Illustrated by Rayanne Vieira

"Kazam! Kazooz!"

Lilly Esther put on her magic cape. Lilly Esther loved her full name, but everyone called her Lilly, except if that person was annoyed. Her sweet Olivia was always by her side!

"I am the Queen of Magic! People everywhere will line up to see me! Kazam, Kazooz!" Olivia and Lilly spun around. She could make a coin disappear. But she wanted to change a ball into a book, her stuffie horse into a real one—she needed an AUDIENCE!

She ran down the stairs calling for Lola, her baby sister. "Hey, Lola! Watch me turn this ball into a—"

"Lilly, I'm busy watching Mr. Baker's Friends on my iPad—maybe later."

Lilly clenched her fists and ran to see Dad in his office.

"Dad, Dad, watch me turn this ball into a—"

"Lilly, can't you see I am busy working at the computer? Please— later," Dad said.

"Grrrr," Lilly grumbled. Mom would listen!

Lilly raced up the stairs to see her mom giving Lola a bath, and Lola was splashing bubbles everywhere!

"Mom!" Lilly said. "Watch me turn this ball into a—"

"Lilly, I can't hear you when Lola is splashing! Please— later!"

Lilly left the bathroom, holding back her tears.

"What can I do to get my family to listen to me? I am the Queen of Magic!" she shouted to the air.

Back in her bedroom, she scooped up her favorite jet. "I wish I could fly anywhere and everywhere."

Lilly picked up her wand.

"Kazam! Kazooz!"

She started spinning around and around. *Faster! Faster!* She became dizzy and started swaying back and forth ... what was happening? POP!

Yikes! She was tiny in her miniature jet with tiny wide-eyed Olivia as her co-pilot. She was flying! Up, Up and all around! Wow! She had to show *THIS* to her family! They would listen now!

Lilly flew to the bathroom. Mom
and Lola were gone. She flew to
the office but Dad was gone, too.
"I bet they are all in the kitchen." In
her loudest tiny voice, Lilly shouted,
"Hey guys! Look out! Here comes the
Queen of Magic!"
Full speed ahead! "I'm coming
into the kitchen!" she called.

But her family didn't **EVEN** notice tiny Lilly flying around in her tiny jet. Lilly landed her jet near the kitchen sink.

"Shhh," Lilly said to Olivia. "Stay here." *But tiny Olivia's bark would be so quiet no one would hear it anyway.*

"Now I can get their attention!" With a wave of her wand, she stopped the water from flowing and crawled up the faucet to hide.

"I can't turn the water on," Mom said. Dad and Lola came running. No water was coming out of the faucet. Dad looked under the sink. Lilly giggled.

"Everything looks fine under the sink," Dad said.

"Hey, where's Lilly?" asked Lola. Where *was* Lilly?

Everyone started shouting, "Lilly, Lilly Esther, where are you? Where *ARE* you?"

Lilly took a deep breath and shouted, "I'm in the faucet."

"Where?" the family said altogether. A little hand emerged from the faucet waving.

"Lilly, is that your *hand?*"

"Yes, it's mine," tiny Lilly said in her loudest tiny voice.

"Please come out!" the family pleaded.

"Why should I? You don't listen to me. I am Lilly Esther,
Queen of Magic!" she said.
"You're right. Please come out," Mom said.

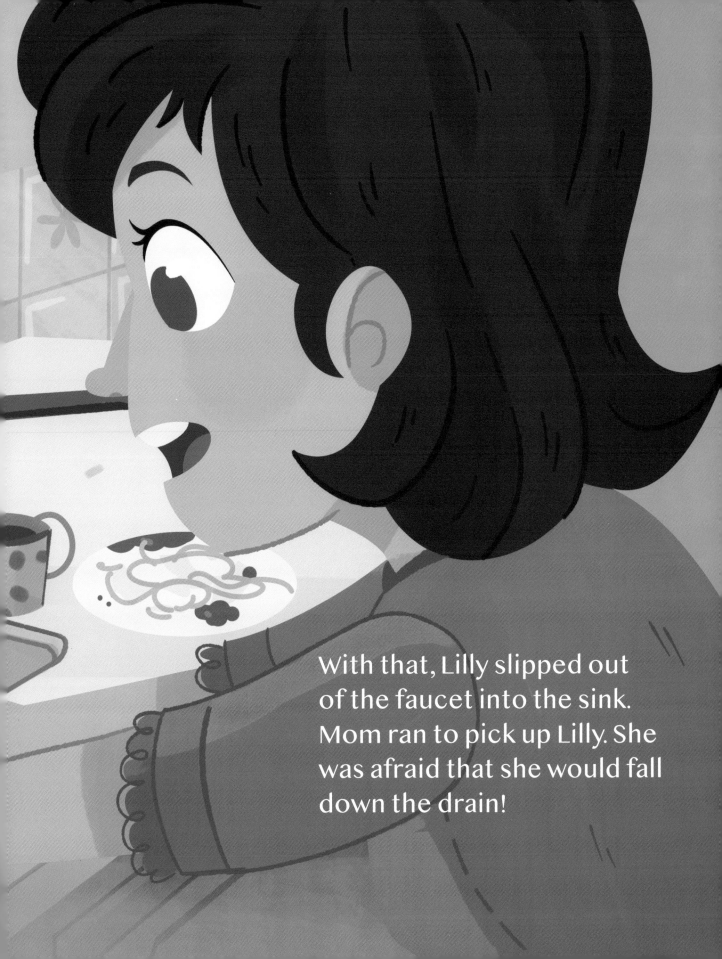

With that, Lilly slipped out of the faucet into the sink. Mom ran to pick up Lilly. She was afraid that she would fall down the drain!

"Lilly, you *CAN* do magic," Lola said as she beamed at her big sister. "Show us more!"

"Watch me turn back to my normal size!" Lilly said.

Lilly's eyes grew wide. *What if I can't change back?*

She jumped out of Mom's hands, ran forward, jumped into her jet, and flew up into the air spinning around. Faster! Faster! With one final spin, she shouted, "Kazam! Kazooz!" Whomp!! Lilly's feet hit the kitchen floor.

Ah! Back to normal!

"Now, watch me turn this ball into a book!
Kazam! Kazooz!"

Waving the magic wand,
Lilly spun around. **POP!** Lilly
was holding Lola's favorite bedtime
storybook. Everyone clapped and cheered.

Mom and Dad finished making dinner while Lilly and Lola set the table. After dinner, Lilly put on the best magic show ever with Olivia as her assistant.

"I am Lilly Esther, the Queen of Magic!"

THE
END

About the Author

Phyllis Bordo is a retired high school English teacher who loves kids and animals. She read to her grandchildren and volunteered at their school library when they were young. Noticing how much these little ones worried about everything, she created the character of Lilly Esther. Phyllis's stories help children find ways to cope with their fears and anxieties, no matter what they are, in a humorous and loving way.

Phyllis lives in Toronto with her husband and two dogs, Lilly Esther and Cleopatra.

Read about more
Lilly Esther
adventures!

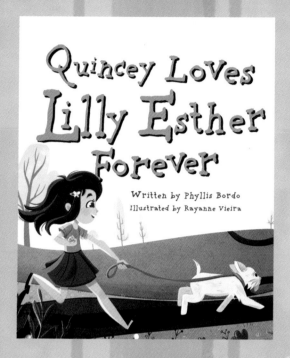

Quincey Loves Lilly Esther Forever

Written by Phyllis Bordo

Illustrated by Rayanne Vieira

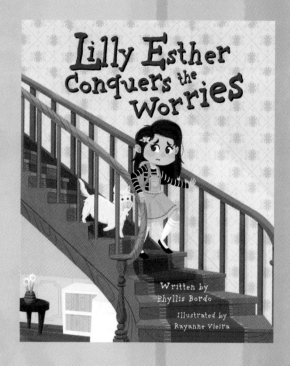

Lilly Esther Conquers the Worries

Written by Phyllis Bordo

Illustrated by Rayanne Vieira

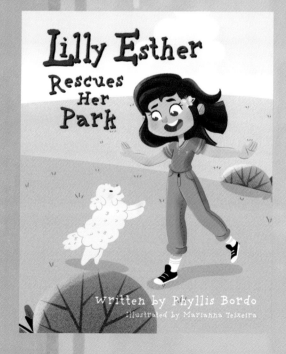

Lilly Esther Rescues Her Park

Written by Phyllis Bordo

Illustrated by Marianna Teixeira